reve

SOPHIE SMILEY

Illustrated by
MICHAEL FOREMAN

This bind-up edition first published in 2010
by Andersen Press Limited
20 Vauxhall Bridge Road
London SW1V 2SA
www.andersenpress.co.uk

The rights of Sophie Smiley and Michael Foreman to be identified as
the author and illustrator of this work have been asserted by them in
accordance with the Copyright, Designs and Patents Act, 1988.

Bobby, Charlton and the Mountain text © Sophie Smiley, 2003
Bobby, Charlton and the Mountain illustration © Michael Foreman, 2003
Man of the Match text © Sophie Smiley, 2005
Man of the Match illustration © Michael Foreman, 2005
Team Trouble text © Sophie Smiley, 2007
Team Trouble illustration © Michael Foreman, 2007

Bobby, Charlton and the Mountain first published in 2003;
Man of the Match first published in 2005; and
Team Trouble first published in 2007, all by Andersen Press.

British Library Cataloguing in Publication Data available.

ISBN 978 184 939 116 0

Printed and bound in Great Britain by CPI Bookmarque, Croydon CR0 4TD

Author's royalties for *Man of the Match* go to the
Camphill Village Trust (Botton Village).

Contents

Bobby, Charlton and the Mountain

For Thomas, William and Piete

Chapter 1

My family is football mad! Mum and Dad are so football crazy they even spent their wedding day at a football match.

Dad asked Mum: "How many kids do you want?"

And she said, "A whole football team!"

When they got to me he said, "Well, we've made it to five-a-side!"

I was born with loads of ginger hair, and Dad started singing, "Come on, you reds!" He was embarrassing even then!

It was Dad's idea to call me Charlton, but everyone calls me Charlie. At school they used to say, "That's a funny name for a girl!" Hardly anyone had heard of my dad's hero, Bobby Charlton. My big brothers are called Wembley, Striker, and Semi (we reached the semifinals that year); then it's Bobby, and last of all, me.

We were brought up on football right from the first whistle. Babies in our house didn't dribble drool: as soon as we could toddle we dribbled footballs! We never had soppy plastic rattles with baby bells: no, we went straight on to big, wooden football rattles. And when we were little, Mum hardly ever shouted at us: if we were naughty she just blew a whistle and produced a yellow card. Two yellow cards meant straight to bed – and NO arguing with the ref! Bobby and I were always getting sent off!

We're a kind of team, Bobby and I, so when he has a problem, it's my problem too.

Well, one Friday Bobby came in gasping: "Queenie comin', Charlie – me's agiving f'owers – got no goalie kit!" The Queen was visiting Bobby's school, and he had been chosen to give her a bouquet; more than anything in the whole world, Bobby wanted to wear his team's goalie kit for the royal appointment!

"Mum . . ." I began. But I already knew what she was going to say – "I'm sorry, Charlie, but we can't afford it. Perhaps when your father . . ."

Dad lost his job when the factory closed. He helps with the football at Bobby's school, but not for money. Bobby's face slipped and his eyes went all swimmy. I couldn't let him down.

"I'll get the money somehow," I told him. "I'll work on it."

Chapter 2

It wasn't until the school fête that I realized Bobby was working on it too.

Bobby was doing "Beat the Goalie". He's the best goalie in his class! I used to get jealous because his school has real goalposts, but we only have traffic cones. And he gets to go by taxi. You see, Bobby goes to a special school cos he's got Down's

syndrome. Mum says we're all
special. Just different.

Well, we were at the school
fête, and Bobby stood in the goal,
running on the spot. He jigged a

bit, then flung himself at the ball
– *whoosh*! – flat out. He never
worries about hurting himself: he
just goes for it – *whoomph*!

In between goals he trotted
over to me, peered in the money
jar, and grinned. All afternoon he
shouted, "'Ow much? 'Ow much
now, Charlie?" But still I didn't
get it. Not till the very end of the
afternoon when he shook the
can and cried, "Nuff for a
goalie top, Charlie?" did
the penny drop: Bobby
thought the money
was for him!

"Nuff now?"

His eyes were all beamy bright. It was like in those cartoons when you see pound signs in people's eyes. Well, I could see goalie kits in Bobby's. I stood there, shaking my head. And his eyes went all cloudy; his face crinkled up, not understanding.

"Goalie kit?" For a second the light in his face swooshed on again.

"No! The money's for the new swimming pool."

"Goalie kit!" he wailed, and shot up the goalpost, wrapping himself round the crossbar.

"I wan' my goalie kit!" he yelled. All these people appeared.

"Ooh dear," they clucked, "poor little lamb – he'll hurt himself!"

14

They were worried about
Bobby hurting himself. I was
worried about getting him down!
Help! What would Mum do?

I grabbed a lolly wrapper,
flashed it at Bobby, and yelled:
"Yellow card!" Bobby glared.

I glared back. The audience carried on clucking.

"I'm going to count to five, and then it'll be the red," I tried. "One, two . . ." Bobby clung on tighter.

Then Dad sailed through the crowd. Phew! He lifted his arms up and said: "Never argue with the ref, Bobs!" Bobby dropped into a big hug and Dad swung him onto his shoulders, saying, "Always accept the ref's decision, and hold your head high!"

They galloped off to throw sponges at a teacher.

I thought it was all over. And I hoped Bobby would forget about the goalie kit. He often forgets

which way round his T-shirt goes,
or when it's his turn to do the
washing up, but some things stick
in his mind like chewing gum.
This was one of them!

Chapter 3

Next morning Bobby and I went shopping. We passed Kevin Joggs from my class. He stuck his tongue out at me, and then pulled his eyes down all slitty and tried to catch Bobby's attention. I felt like kicking him you-know-where, but I could hear Dad's "Hold your head high, and walk away". So I grabbed Bobby's arm and shouted, "Look, Bobby! Come

and see the one-man band!"
   Brilliant save, I thought . . .
   Bobby sat on the pavement
cross-legged, and rocked happily.

The music man drummed away. Bobby's fingers waggled on his knees in time to the music. He's got lovely waggly fingers that all move at different times. I don't know anyone who's got fingers like Bobby's. Two white mice ran round the rim of the man's top hat, and Bobby's eyes went as round as circles as he watched.

Then a new problem hit me: how was I going to get Bobby away from the busker? My brilliant save was turning into an own goal . . . I gave Bobby some pennies. He slipped them into his pocket and said, "Goalie top!"

"No – put them in the hat!"

"Goalie?" he begged.

I bobbed beneath the white mice and whispered in the music man's ear. He winked at me, and galloped into "Oh When the Saints . . ."

Then he tipped his hat to Bobby, saying: "Here's to you, young 'un. I've got to be going now."

"Me's goin' to see the Queen," Bobby said proudly.

"Well, don't chase any mice under her chair!" he replied, holding out a mouse for Bobby to stroke.

Chuckling, Bobby dropped the coins in the hat. But he did look at that hat in a very odd way . . .

It was quiet when we got back home. Dad had taken the big ones to an all-day tournament, and Mum was helping Gran. I made sandwiches, listening to the babble of Bobby's "Best Goals" video from the back room. He watches that video over and over.

I'd just about finished when I realized something was wrong . . . badly wrong. The whole house had gone quiet. It was the sort of quiet you get while waiting for a penalty. That special sort of quiet which tells me Bobby's up to mischief or . . . in trouble. I ran from the kitchen. The front door was wide open. The street was empty. Should I go looking, or

phone Mum? The police? I heard
a siren, and felt sick.

Tearing down the street I
scanned the side roads frantically.
Traffic roared from the main
road. What if he'd tried to cross?
It was really fast – he wasn't
allowed there by himself . . . I ran
faster, gasping. How would I tell
Mum? My feet pounded the
pavement, my eyes stung. At the
junction a massive lorry
thundered by. Two boy racers
screeched their brakes. Another
siren wailed. I turned. My
stomach somersaulted at the sight
before me: a huge crowd gathered
by the shops. They were grouped
round something. An accident?

Bobby! I tore up to them, smudging away tears with my jersey.

"Let me through!" I pulled wildly at the people. "It's my brother, it's . . ."

The crowd parted, and there, on the pavement, was . . .

"Bobby?" I gulped.

He was wearing Mum's pink wedding hat, the one with roses round the rim, dangling a tambourine, twiddling a football rattle, and banging an old Coke tin. Looking at me with his biggest crack-your-face-in-half grin, he said, "'Ello, Charlie!"

Everyone was smiling: great, stupid, happy smiles. And I just stood there with tears running down my cheeks.

Bobby belted out a mixture of football songs, stringing together all his favourite bits: "Football's comin' 'ome, it's comin' 'ome" – a bit of humming and tambourine crashing – "Swing low, sweet Charlie 'ot" and ending up with "Oh whe' the sai'ts go munching in . . ."

The crowd clapped, sang along and tossed coins into the bobble hat at Bobby's feet.

Well, Mum laughed till the tears ran down her face when I told her the story! Bobby did a repeat performance for the family, and loved every minute of it!

Chapter 4

But I felt pretty fed up as I set off for school the next day: the Queen's visit was getting nearer, and I was no closer to getting his kit. Even if I saved up all my pocket money I'd still only have enough for a pair of football socks!

"We're going to start a new project on letter writing," Ms Stadia announced in literacy hour. Boring or what?! I stared out of the window.

"I want you all to write to someone famous. We'll see if we get any replies!"

That was the starting whistle! Kick off! I couldn't write fast enough: "Dear Mr Brooks," – I had to write to Bobby's favourite goalie! I told him how Bobby has his pictures all round the house, and how he runs around like an aeroplane whenever he watches a save, and all about the Queen coming to his school, and the busking expedition . . . Ms Stadia said I was a bit short on full stops, but she smiled. I think she liked it. At the end I put: "P.S. It's

Bobby's birthday on the thirtieth. Mum says we shouldn't ask for things, but I know he'd be dead chuffed if you sent him a photograph."

Well, other people started getting replies. But nothing came to our house.

Every morning I rushed downstairs to meet the postman, hoping and hoping. And every morning there'd be a little pile of brown bills. Never mind, he might still send a birthday card, I told myself. I could hardly sleep the night before Bobby's birthday, and in the morning I leaped down and sat on the doormat, waiting. The flap opened; cards

plopped onto my lap. I flipped
through them, really excited. But
it wasn't there. No club crest.
Nothing.

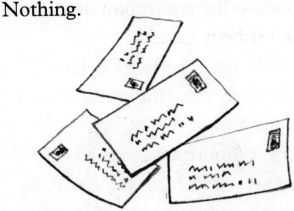

"Wadsamatter, Charlie?" Bobby
asked when he saw me, and I
tried to smile. I tried really hard
to be cheerful, but Mum could
see I was moping. She'd knitted
him a jumper in club colours. It
was really nice, and he liked it.
But I was still disappointed.

"Cheer up," Mum said, giving me a hug. "There's still second post. Now why don't you go down to the rec while I decorate the birthday cake?"

I always feel better once I'm on a football pitch. Bobby went in goal. Jigging. I used to think that his jigging was magic, that it told him which way to dive.

Kevin Joggs pressed his face against the netting. "Nice jumper," he said sarcastically. "Yer mum knit it?"

Bobby was too busy watching the ball to notice. I started to run up, and when I was just a metre away, Kevin yelled: "Girls are useless – they can't kick straight!"

I looked up for a second, and lost my rhythm. I was too close. I kicked with my left. And I knew as I watched the ball loop in slow motion where it would end.

"Post, post." Kevin was jumping up and down. "Girly whirly post!" he chanted. "Told you girls can't play!"

Bobby swung round. "Charlie's good!" he said angrily.

"Call that good?" Kevin sneered. "A monkey could kick better than that!"

'Bobby, don't . . .' I called as he moved forward, clenching his hands. 'Please, Bobby, don't fight!'

Bobby walked right up to the netting.

He's going to hit him! I ran forward.

"You watch," Bobby shouted. "She gooder 'an you."

He lifted his chin and turned away really calmly, collected the ball, and passed it to me. I was so proud.

"You show 'im, Charlie."

I stepped back. Measured the run up. This one had to be good. I wanted it to power into the back of the net out the other side and right into Kevin's sneery smile. I trotted up slowly. Stay calm. Foot back. *Pow!*

"OK?" I said to Kevin, casual but pleased. "See?"

"Mongrel," he hissed, "your brother's a mongrel . . ."

"He is NOT!" I growled. "He's the best goalie in his school – now push off!"

He moved away, but then turned and smiled at Bobby, an awful, sickly smile.

He cooed, "You are a mongrel, aren't you? Tell your silly sister you're a mongrel."

"Charlie . . ." Bobby began, all desperate. He knew the smiling was nasty, but he couldn't understand it. His eyes were really hurting, begging.

I went bananas!

I hurled myself. Kevin didn't even see me coming. I floored him – flat on his fat belly. My fists hammered his back, hammering out that cooing voice.

"Stop, Charlie, stop!" Bobby

tugged. Kevin grunted. I pushed
his face into the mud.

"No fightin', Charlie – head
high!"

I went limp. Bobby was right.
I'd let Dad down. Staggering to

my feet, I fought to hold back
hot tears.

"Beat him a' football, Charlie,"
he nodded towards the goal.
"Football . . ."

"Challenge you to a shoot-
out!" I said loudly and coldly. He
looked around. A clump of other
children had gathered.

"Go on," said Jamie. "She's only a girl – even you could beat her."

"Yeah, all right," Kevin said. "Yeah – I'll show her."

He stuck his chest out, but there was a slight wobble in his walk. He ran up and walloped the ball into the top corner. A perfect penalty. He swaggered to the side.

"You go in goal," he said to Jamie. "Her brother'd cheat!"

"Go, Charlton!" one of the girls called. "You can do it!"

I looked at the goal. The ball. I ran forward, gaining speed, and kicked. It was in! A cheer went up.

The next couple went in. Two all. Level pegging. Kevin went for his third. Bobby knew which way it was coming. He dived brilliantly. His finger caught it, held it for a second. But it curled in. Bobby slunk off, and sat in a heap, hands over his head.

"Walk tall," I whispered, as I lined up, feeling very small.

I hit hard and straight. But Jamie was there.

"Yees!" Jamie yelled. "Three – two! You've lost!"

No one else cheered.

"It's best of five, anyway," called Alison.

Kevin ran forward, full of confidence, and slammed the ball. It looked unstoppable. But then, somehow, Bobby was across the goal mouth, punching the ball away. A cheer rose from the sidelines.

My chance to equalize!

Worse than any of the other run ups. It had to go in . . . At the

very last second I saw Jamie
move. In a snap moment I
changed foot, changed plan, and
watched the ball sail the opposite
way to the goalie. It crashed into
the post.

"Ohh . . ." went the group. It
bounced . . . and landed just
inside the line!

"Ahhh . . ." went the crowd.

I was back with a chance!

Everyone was still for the last round, except Bobby, who jigged a little more than usual. His face was crinkled up in concentration. There was just him and the ball. The ball flew. Bobby flew. Thud! He smashed it out!

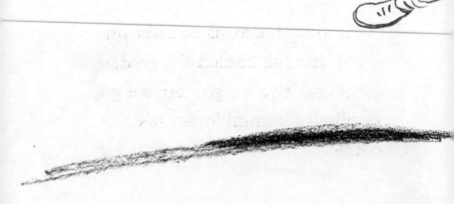

Holding his arms out like an
aeroplane, he circled the goal,
singing, "'Ere we go, 'ere we go,
Football's comin' 'ome, It's
comin' . . ."

"You've done it, Charlie," Rasheda shouted. But I hadn't done it. Not yet. This one had to go in. This shot was for all the girls in the world, and for Bobby not fighting . . .

I stood still for ages. A tall figure loped in our direction, but I shut him out. I shut out the ring of spectators, and even blotted out Bobby, who was watching through split fingers. There was just me and those posts. This time there could be no risks, no last minute changes . . . I ran, looked, kicked and . . . closed my eyes.

"Waddagoal! Waddagoal!" Bobby's voice rang over the cheers.

I sank to my knees, exhausted.
A huge shadow fell across me.
Mountainous. I stared up. The
mountain was jigging from foot
to foot, like Bobby does. And
grinning a little, jiggy smile, like
Bobby when he's nervous.

"Charlie?" Will Brooks' voice
was deep and warm. "Your
mother said I'd find you here –
I've brought a birthday card for
Bobby . . ."

"Yees!" I shrieked, pulling my elbows down and my fists up. "Yees!!"

Before I could blurt out my thanks, Bobby ran towards us. He took one look at the smiling mountain, and flung himself, all arms and legs, around his favourite goalie hero!

"Waddasave, waddasave!" he yelled, and together they twirled round the rec singing, "Oh when the sai'ts go munching in . . ."

It was brilliant!

Then Dad arrived and started doing his vindaloo war dance. Embarrassing or what? But even that didn't spoil Bobby's big day. Mum arrived with the cake, and

the older ones clutched autograph books.

Bobby sat with his birthday card. He gazed and gazed at the team photo. He didn't even notice the sports bag, until someone prodded him and pointed. Even then, he didn't understand that it was for him! His eyes were as wide as footballs when he unzipped it and found – a brand new goalie kit with 'BOBBY' in big letters on the back.

He stared and stared . . . Putting out one finger he touched it, and pulled away quickly as if it were hot. Then he put out another finger and stroked it gently, like a fragile creature.

All his fingers began to waggle
up and down in the silky fabric,
before he scooped it to him,
hugging and rocking and smiling.
It was the best birthday ever!

Chapter 5

And now, for the first time in my life, I'm sitting down to write a thank-you letter without Mum nagging me! At the top I've done a crest – like the ones you get on cereal packets. It says: "Bobby: by appointment to H.M. the Queen." Underneath I've drawn a picture of him all dressed up in his goalie kit. The Queen is beaming at him and holding his

bunch of flowers. The flowers are
smiling. Bobby's smile is so big
it's banging into his ears – almost
booting his ears into the goal.
Even the ball is grinning!

"Dear Mr" I begin; then I
tippex out the Mr and write
"Dear Will". We're on first name
terms, now, Bobby's goalie
mountain and me!

Man of
the Match

To Timothy and Benita Smiley,
and Victor and Greta Brooks

Chapter 1

"Camping?" Bobby banged my bunk with both feet.

"Not today!"

"Tents?"

"No. Go back to sleep."

Every morning, for a whole week, he woke me. He was all jittery, like a goalie waiting for a free kick. We were waiting to go to Special Camp – a holiday for children with special needs and

their siblings. That's me. Bobby's
sister. His sibling. Bobby loved
that word. When he first heard it,
he ran round the room yelling,
"Sib-ling, sib-ling," like a fire
engine.

At last the big day arrived.
Bobby woke me at three o'clock.
And four o'clock. And five
o'clock. By six o'clock he was all
dressed up in his beloved goalie
top, and raring to go!

We set off for Bobby's school.
It's different from mine because
he's got Down's syndrome. I used
to get jealous, as he goes in a taxi.
Once, I even asked, "Mum, why
can't I go to a special school?"

She said, "You're special just as

you are. We need a girl on our team." You see, my mum and dad are so football mad that they wanted enough children for a football team. They ended up with a five-a-side: Wembley, Semi, Striker, Bobby and me! My daft dad gave us all football names. Bobby and I are called after his World Cup hero, Bobby Charlton. Some people think Charlton's a funny first name, but I think it's lucky; perhaps I'll be the first girl to play in a World Cup final!

Well, that Saturday, the whole team was there to wave us off. Wembley swung Bobby round by his ankles, Semi twirled a football rattle, and Striker dribbled a ball

in and out of the bags, did a
nutmeg round the driver and
scored a goal through the coach!

Looking around the
playground, I recognized nearly
everyone. Most of the helpers had
been on the holiday play scheme.
Laura, a pretty girl from Bobby's

class, was clinging to her mother. Her brother, Sean, hissed, "Baby," then pinched her when he thought no one was looking. I was glad he wasn't my brother.

There was just one boy, by himself, who didn't go to Bobby's school. It was a hot day, but he was wearing a coat with fur round the hood. His head was bowed, as if he didn't want to look at anyone. Bobby noticed him too, and went over.

"'Ello," he said.

There was no response. Bobby put his head on one side, leaned close and said, "'Ello," again. He looked around, and asked, "Sib-ling?" He expected everyone on the camp to have a sister, like he had.

A grey-haired woman stepped forward. "This is Paul. I'm his care worker. He doesn't talk. Perhaps you'll keep an eye on him for me?"

Bobby put an arm around

Paul's shoulder and said, "Friends?"

But Paul shuffled away from the hug, and stared at his trainers.

"C'mon, Paul." Bobby beckoned him onto the coach. Paul followed at a distance, flicking his hood strings. As we pulled out of the playground, Wembley, Semi and Striker ran along trying to keep up with us. Mum shouted, "Don't forget to write," and Dad sang, "Here we go, here we go, here we go!"

The care worker made for her car, and Paul pulled his hood right down over his nose.

Straightaway Bobby began unpacking his lunchbox.

"San'wich, Paul? Crisps? . . .
Biscuit? . . ."

Paul just flicked his hood
toggles faster and faster, while
Bobby ate the whole packed
lunch before we'd even left town!
Every time one of the staff walked
down the coach, Bobby's face lit

up and he asked, "Football? Beat the goalie?" and they answered vaguely, "We're going to do lots of great things. Games. Music. Drama."

I had this funny feeling that their ideas about what to do at camp, and Bobby's, might not be quite the same.

You see, Bobby had set his heart on spending the whole camp doing nothing but football. And I think he'd already decided to make Paul his man of the match.

Chapter 2

Dear Mum and Dad,

It was difficult to write, all squashed up in my little tent, but I knew Mum would be leaping out and doing terrifying tackles on the postman until he brought her a letter from us.

The food is funny, the helpers are cool, and there are spiders in my tent!

When we arrived Bobby danced onto the camp site, with his kitbag on his head, and his arms flapping up and down! Expect you can guess what he did next. Yup! You're right.

Go straight to the top of the Premier League! He built a goalpost. Well, his first one was made of tent poles. But then Tom (d'you remember the helper from play scheme – with the wacky hair?) made him hang a tent over them, and put his sleeping bag in. So next, he got hold of two lanterns. There was this terrible sound of glass breaking – Paul had hit the "post". Then, just before supper, they were taking shots at the back of an old truck when the farmer's dog leaped out. Bobby jumped into Tom's arms, and didn't let go of his hand till bedtime!

Last night I had a nightmare about Bobby building goalposts everywhere, and they started coming to get me! When I woke up, I went to wake Paul and Bobby, but their tent was empty. Paul's pyjamas were folded all neatly, but – surprise, surprise – Bobby's stuff was spread across the field. Just like home. I picked up his teddy and towel and stuff – they were in a trail leading to the river. You'll know how I felt as I got nearer, and heard the water. There were these two posts, right at the edge, and I had this picture of Bobby shouting, "Save!" and diving over the bank. I got all panicky, and started calling his name. Then Tom came along and told me that Paul and Bobby were helping Chris with the breakfast. The "goal" was just two rotten old fence posts – doh!

Rushing over to the kitchen I found Bobby serving. He was holding this bottle of food colouring, dishing out dollops of porridge (bright RED porridge), and singing, "Come on, you reds!"

After breakfast there was music and games, but not football. Bobby wasn't pleased. He had that "I'm planning something" look on his face. I was keeping an eye on him until Sean came over and said, "Bet you can't climb that tree." He went first – boasting about how great he was – and got stuck! Tom had to rescue him – ha ha. Then Fizza and I went up. We got so high the camp looked titchy. I spotted these two trees miles and miles away, with someone

in between them. I was sure it was
Bobby in his latest goal. Fizza said I
needed glasses – it was only a
scarecrow! Then I saw something red
floating down the river, and I nearly
fell out of the tree. I thought it was
Bobby in his goalie top. Fizza
laughed and said it was just an oil
drum. She thinks I'm nutty – she
says she doesn't see her brother, Ali,
popping up all over the place.

I stopped shaking when we got to
the top. It was brilliant. All the
matchstick people waved at us.
Fizza teased me on the way down –
she kept pointing to a sheep, or a
bird and shouting, "Look, it's
Bobby!" and "There's a football
stadium!" Then, just when she'd

convinced me not to see another
phantom goalpost ever, I heard
Bobby shout, "Shoot, Paul, shoot!"

You'll never guess where his new
goal was. Right in front of the serving
table. Well, Paul kicked. Bobby dived.
The ball hit a table leg and the pot of
stew wobbled over the edge.

Bobby wasn't a bit bothered. He

just lay in the grass, with the dinner
trickling past his nose, waggling his
fingers in the gravy and licking
them. Chris caught the pot and yelled
"Save!" while Janet said, "Don't get
in a stew, Chris!" and then Tom
started singing our football anthem,
but changed the words, so it was:

"And STEW'll never walk alone!"

Since then, Bobby's been dribbling a ball round the field, singing, "Stew'll never walk alone" at the top of his voice. He made us all sing it at campfire.

Write and tell me the midweek score, and how Semi's team got on.

Lots of love,

Charlie

PS   Q: *What do you call a nervous camper?*

       A: *TENTS!*

PPS   Q: *What do you call a serious camper?*

       A: *In TENTS!*

PPPS Q: *What do you give an unhappy camper?*

       A: *AtTENTion!*

Chapter 3

After I'd put my letter in the camp postbox, I said goodnight to Bobby. He was half in and half out of his sleeping bag, like a Jack-in-the-box, while Paul was tucked right in, with the drawstring pulled tight round his face. I didn't mind sleeping on my own. I'm not afraid of the dark. Not afraid of anything, me – well, perhaps just one thing. But anyway, I liked the sound of the wind rustling in the trees, and the canvas flapping, and I was soon fast asleep.

Early in the morning I had a dream of a spider dancing up and down my arm. It danced quicker and quicker. And the tune it was dancing to was somehow familiar. It reminded me of . . .

"Bobby?" I called out.

Sure enough, Bobby's hand had slid under the tent door and his fingers were pattering in panic on my arm!

"Charlie," a small voice whimpered from outside. I struggled to unzip the tent. He was shivering and his lower lip was beginning to wobble.

"Moo," a cow bellowed.

Bobby leaped into my tent and dived down the sleeping bag.

"Moooo," went the cow, even louder, and Bobby's head disappeared. I started humming "You'll Never Walk Alone." Gradually Bobby stopped shaking, and I could feel him relax to our football anthem:

I got to the words "And don't be afraid of the . . ." when Bobby jumped in.

"Cows!" he said.

So I sang it again, "And don't be afraid of the cows."

Bobby began to join in. I came to the last bit and as I sang it Bobby giggled and sang out his own final line:

"Moooo'll ne-ver walk a-lone!"

Even the cows joined in his chorus!

Five minutes later he was sound asleep.

Chapter 4

When the gong clanged, I had to shake Bobby awake. And he was still sleepy after breakfast as we all sat round. Only Paul wasn't part of the big circle: he hovered a little way away, not looking at anyone. Dave, one of the adults, stood up. He was big and bearded, and wore a ballet tutu over his jeans! Bobby hid his head in embarrassment, while Dave twirled, waved a magic wand, and announced: "Today we're going to do painting and weaving."

"Beat the goalie?" Bobby asked.

"Perhaps later."

Bobby's face fell. I held my breath, waiting for what might happen. But he only muttered grumpily, and followed me to the craft area.

"Look, Bobby." I cut a potato in half. "You can print footballs on your bag."

Blob, blob, blob he went, making a wall of heads. Blob, blob, blob went the potato, in a Beckham banana kick. Pow! And Bobby was off to the painting.

Paul worked more slowly. He

covered every centimetre of his bag with neat lines, each circle placed carefully, one above the other.

Laura couldn't manage printing, but she laughed as Tom helped her swoosh a paintbrush. Her brother watched. Leaving his printing, he walked past casually, kicking a pot of water over her paper as he went by. I glared at him, and he said "Accident," all innocent. I was about to stick a leg out to trip him, when Bobby stepped in.

"'Ere you are, Laura," he said, holding out a new piece of paper. "Paint it red."

Then he went to have a go at weaving. Janet held out two sticks and Bobby wound wool around them. It was fiddly work, and he soon left it and wandered off, with Paul following like a silent shadow. I could hear him singing "Three lions on my shirt" as I printed a bag for Mum. She always says, "Everything's fine if Bobby is singing. It's when he stops you have to watch out."

As I pressed the last potato, the singing stopped. There was a noisy silence spreading from beyond the tents, the kind of quiet that deafens a stadium before a penalty.

I scrambled up, to find out where it was coming from. Hurrying past the kitchen fire, and up the hill, I reached Bobby's tent. He was so absorbed in his work that he didn't notice me approach. I stood and watched his fingers flying in and out. Paul walked behind him carrying balls of wool – oranges and yellows, and some sparkling with gold thread. Bobby wove the wool between the tent and a tree, up to a washing line, and down to the tent pegs. It was the strangest, most wonderful goalpost I'd ever seen!

Finally, he turned to Paul, and said proudly, "I's a golden goal, Paul!"

And I thought I saw Paul's hood move, just a little, as he darted a look at Bobby's creation.

"Shoot, Paul, shoot!" Bobby
urged.

With his head down, and his
fingers flicking, Paul kicked the
ball to the left. Bobby threw

himself – whoomph – flat out,
hands and feet flying through the
air, through the goal, and into the
tent! The canvas collapsed around
him, and Bobby disappeared.

Paul stood on the spot, rocking anxiously from foot to foot while the tent staggered. It lurched, and fell forward. Then it tumbled down the hill – a twirling, golden meteor, coming to a halt in a circle of surprised people. It chuckled. A set of fingers emerged – fluttering, waggly fingers, playing their own special music.

Then out popped Bobby's head. He grinned and asked, "Football, anyone?"

Paul loped across the grass. Perhaps I was imagining things, but I thought I noticed a slight nod come from inside his tightly tied hood.

Chapter 5

"We're off to see the farm today," Chris announced next morning.

Bobby shook his head fiercely.

"You'll like it," Janet said. "There might be some lambs."

"Football," Bobby said.

"Not now. Everyone's going to the farm."

The rest of the camp gathered by the footpath.

Bobby sat down and I knew

that a battle was about to begin.

Tom came over to see what was wrong. "Come on," he called, "there'll be a treasure hunt."

Bobby buried his head in his crossed legs.

"Football!" he said.

"You can kick a football along the path," Tom tried. "Perhaps the farmer's got a dog who takes penalties."

Bobby didn't move.

"Penalties here!" He wasn't budging.

What would Mum do? Grabbing a plastic plate, I flashed it in front of him, and said, "Red card!" in my firmest voice.

There was a muffled, "Not

goin'," and I knew it was useless.

He was a striker on strike.

"Come on, Charlie – leave him," said Fizza. Everyone else was moving off. I was desperate to follow, but it's hard when you're a team.

"You go on," said Tom. "I'll stay with him."

I turned to go, but my feet wouldn't move. I was going to miss the treasure hunt, the animals, the special tea.

"It's not fair," I said crossly. The grown-ups huddled round Bobby, an anxious team round an injured player. Wordless. Not knowing what to try next.

Then Paul moved. He'd been

standing so quietly that I hadn't even noticed him. Like a good striker, he always had his own pool of space. Now he edged towards Bobby. Surprised, everyone else moved back. Paul crept forwards, taking tiny steps. He hovered above Bobby, rocking. Bobby didn't move, but I could tell he knew Paul was there. The toggles of Paul's coat swung, gently ruffling Bobby's hair. Two eyes peeped out. The toggles moved faster. Bobby's fingers pattered. Then, like a swimmer bursting for air, Paul started running off across the grass. Startled, Bobby looked round, scrambled to his feet, and

followed. Sometimes, a player works some magic on a pitch, and you just blink and think, "How did he do that?" Well, we all stood, staring after the disappearing figures, blinking!

Paul and Bobby arrived at the farm passing a ball between them. They were greeted by the farmer's wife who gave everyone baskets, and sent us off on an egg hunt. For a few minutes Bobby forgot about playing football and dashed about between the barn and the yard, searching through piles of hay.

"Look over here," I called.

When he saw the speckled, brown hen's egg his face crumpled.

He shook his head, saying, "Not real!"

"Yes, it is." I passed it to him. He licked it gingerly, and then, before I could stop him, he took a big bite! Golden goo exploded everywhere, and Bobby spat in disgust.

"Not chocolate!" He looked at me accusingly.

And it was only then I realized that Bobby thought we were hunting for Easter eggs!

Wiping his mouth, he sloped
off to get some target practice
against a wall. I could hear the
ball thud as I sat eating a cream
tea in the farmer's garden. The
strawberry jam was thick and
gloopy on the crumbly scones. I
soaked up the sun and the scene
and the . . . SILENCE! I
remembered Mum's words.

Where was Bobby?

Suddenly, Paul tore past and clambered frantically onto a tractor.

There was a scream!

I stood up and gaped in horror at Bobby's latest goal. He had opened the five-bar gate. And there he was, frozen, in the middle of his open gate-goal.

And standing in front of him was the ugliest, hairiest striker I'd ever seen! It lowered its head to the ground, hunched its huge shoulders and snorted. Flying forwards, it hurtled towards Bobby. Then, with a quick flick of its horns, it tossed the ball up, past Bobby, and into his goal.

Bobby didn't even see the ball.

His eyes were glued to the bull.
It banged a hoof in applause, then
trotted off to join a crowd of
spectating cows.

Bobby walked backwards in a
wobbly way, picked up his
precious football, then sprinted
up behind Paul on the tractor.
The red-faced farmer dashed
across and clanged the gate shut.
Paul pushed back his hood, and
turned the steering wheel round
and round, while Bobby swung
the gear stick. A wobbly wail
floated from the tractor:

"And don't be afraid of the
cows."

Everyone in the farmyard
started joining in, and our

football anthem filled the air.
"You'll Never Walk Alone"!

The colour flooded back into Bobby's face, and his voice swelled across the farmyard in his favourite refrain:

"Moooooooo'll neeeeeeeeever walk aloooooone!"

Chapter 6

I'm pretty brave about most
things: spiders, heights, bullies. I
can usually take care of anything.
But there was one place at camp
I'd avoided all week – until the
last afternoon.

I was busy carving a totem pole
with Fizza when Chris
announced, "Water sports at the
river!"

The river! My heart pounded

as I remembered the day Kevin Joggs pushed me into the deep end of the swimming pool. I have these nightmares where I struggle to breathe and thrash about, desperate to get out. Then I wake, and Mum's there, all the blankets on the floor, and me gasping for air.

"Water sports!" Chris repeated.

For the first time since we'd left home I wanted Mum. Really wanted her, so badly I could feel a knot in my stomach. I'll go to my tent – pretend to be poorly, I thought.

I was just about to slink away, when Janet walked up. "You've got some post," she grinned. The envelope was covered in Dad's cartoon drawings of our favourite players. Still trembling at the thought of the water, I ripped it open.

Dear Charlie,

Thanks for your letter. Glad you're both conTENT at camp.

It was my inTENTion to clear the shed while you were away, but I found a set of Bobby's football annuals in there, and I'm reading them instead! I'm planning – TENTatively – to paint your room. Mum will show me the red card if I don't!

We won 2–0 on Tuesday –
great save by Will Brooks –
and Semi's team drew 3–3,
equalizing in the ninetieth
minute.

Love, Dad

***PS Q:** What does an octopus*
defender do in a game
of camp football?

***A:** A TENT-tackle!*

Oh Dad! He can always make me
laugh, and suddenly I missed him
so much. He would know how
scared I was.

But getting his card made me
see something else. Dad would
never pretend to be ill to get out
of something. He'd never run

105

away. It would be like those players who fake injury to get a penalty. We don't have any time for them in our house. I fought back tears, feeling sick at the very thought of the water, but not wanting to let Dad down.

Then there was a slight fluttering on my arm. A light pattering. No words, just the rhythm of gently drumming fingers.

"Bobby!"

There are some things Bobby understands better than anyone else. So when he tugged my hand, I followed him down to the bank.

Two logs spanned the river. In the first game, people had to walk across a plank, carrying a mug of water, and empty it in a bucket on the other side. Chris asked for volunteers, and the two teams lined up. I sloped off to sit with the spectators. Bobby was jigging up and down, eager to start, but his team didn't have enough players.

"We need one more person," Chris called out.

I knew I couldn't do it, not over all that water.

"C'mon, Charlie," Fizza called.

I shook my head.

"Scaredy cat, scaredy cat!" Sean shouted.

That did it! My knees wobbled as I stood up. And I thought, this

is how it must feel in a World
Cup penalty shoot-out. You step
up, and the whole world is
watching you, and your heart's
banging out an anthem of terror!

"Be all right." Bobby patted my
arm.

And the next moment, the race
started! Tom and Jacob, wearing

silly dresses, flippers and snorkels,
set off! They trotted across easily.
Bobby went next for our team. He
walked backwards across the log,
arms flapping, and the water in his
mug wobbling. Reaching the far
side, he skipped off the log and
took a bow! Everyone cheered. We
were well ahead when Max began.

He went too fast, and almost at once – splash – he was in the water. He paddled back to the bank and started again. This time he crept across with tiny tiptoe steps, and two of the other team overtook him. Then it was Chonka's turn. He sat on the log, and pulled himself forward on his bottom, holding the mug between his teeth. Across from him Nadia fell in three times, and we began to draw level – until there were just two people left: Sean and me.

The water was murky. I could hear Dad's voice saying, "Hold your head up high!"

A much louder voice in MY head said, "Sharks!"

But I made myself step onto the
log.

"Swim low, sweet Charlie 'ot,"
Bobby sang from the opposite
bank.

I kept my eyes glued to Bobby's
face; he willed me on. I was
halfway across when a huge spray
of water soaked me. Sean had
fallen in. I'd be next. I froze.
Couldn't go on. Couldn't go back.
The water in my mug trembled. I
started shaking. Any second now
and . . .

"Splosh!" There were thrashing
sounds. My knees were giving way.

"'S all right, Charlie, 's all right."

There, below me in the water,
rushing to my rescue, was Bobby.

"One step, Charlie, tha's right."

My foot inched forward.

"One step, two step, tickly under there," Bobby sang as he swam along beside me. "Big step, Charlie!"

I didn't look across at Sean, but I could sense it was a photo finish. We were level. It felt like the eighty-ninth minute of a match. I had to score. I flung myself forward onto the mud, and a great cheer went up. Bobby scrambled up the bank, shook water over everyone, then jumped onto me, all arms and legs, and together we twirled around the field singing "We are the champions!"

Chapter 7

Bobby looked at the buckets where everyone had emptied their mugs. The two FULL buckets of water. Glancing around like a pantomime villain, he picked up a bucket, crept up behind Tom, and threw the water over him! Tom grabbed the other bucket and soaked Bobby; soon everyone was joining in a massive water fight. It only stopped when Chris called out: "What do you call the thing that carries electricity?"

"A pylon?" said Tom.

"That's right – PILE ON!" and everyone piled on top of Tom!

The afternoon continued with water slides, water pistols and raft building. Bobby joined in each activity, but every few minutes his voice piped up like a referee's whistle. "Football?"

And one of the helpers would say, "Not now. It's water sports today."

Bobby scowled.

There was a lull before tea. "Sleeping lions!" someone shouted, and we all lay in a line with our heads on each other's tummies. The first person giggled, and a rippling roar of laughter zigzagged down the chain. I listened for Bobby's chuckle. Strange. I glanced around at all the bouncing heads and bellies. No Bobby. I scanned the field for his mop of red hair, for Paul's hunched, hooded figure. It was empty! I got up and hurried across the grass, through the cowpats and nettles, and back to the water. The river coiled like a snake. The water was dark and murky where we'd stirred it up. I strained to see through the darkness.

I looked around wildly. There, in the distance, walking beside the willows, was a figure on its own. It looked familiar, but strange: a boy in jeans and a T-shirt. Then I realized. It was Paul. Paul, WITHOUT his coat! But where was Bobby?

"Paul," I called, trying to keep the panic from my voice. "Where's . . ."

Tom emerged from behind Paul. He seemed to be watching the water. What was he staring at?

Seconds later, Bobby floated round the corner and sailed into sight. He was standing astride a raft, dressed in his swimming trunks and goalie top, waving a football rattle.

Tom, hovering in the background, gave me a thumbs-up sign. And I realized he'd been with them all the time, watching.

And I realized, too, that Mum was right when she said, "You don't have to look after him, Charlie."

By now, everyone had gathered

to watch Bobby's triumphal entry.
A kingfisher shot in front of him,
a turquoise striker zipping
through the defence. Bobby threw
a football at Paul and announced:
"It's water football time!"

Paul kicked from the bank, and
Bobby flung himself – whoomph
– flat out, grabbing the ball before

crashing into the water. He emerged, draped in reeds and weeds and water lilies, spurting a great fountain from his mouth and chanting, "Whaddasave, whaddasave!" He leaped and stretched, soared and dived until the dinner gong went. And that afternoon, Bobby kept a clean, but very wet, sheet!

Chapter 8

"Mooo . . ." The cows woke me early on the last morning. I waited for a frightened Bobby to leap into my tent. Instead, I heard him bellowing, "Moo off, cows!"

After a farewell hokey cokey, we trudged up the hill towards the coach. Bobby darted round the cowpats, pretending he was dodging defenders in a run on goal. As he rounded the brow of the hill, Tom and Jacob leaped out, wearing top hats and waving magic wands. A row of children and adults were lined up like a wall of defenders; they were hiding something.

Tom waved his tent-pole wand, and chanted:

"Abracca dabracca, Abracca dole,

Turn this tent pole into a . . . GOAL!"

Everyone moved aside to reveal a magical, end-of-camp goalpost! The uprights were made from the farmer's crooks. Ballet tutus, potato print flags and flippers dangled from the crossbar! The staff started singing, "There was

Bobby, Bobby, mad about his hobby, in the stores," as Tom said, "For our last trick we have our very own Beat the Goalie competition!"

Jacob snipped a pink ribbon and declared the goal officially open. We all lined up for our shots, and Bobby flew across that goal front like Superman! He saved every shot.

Paul lined up last. "Shoot, Paul, shoot!" Bobby shouted.

All week Paul had run up with his head turned away from the goal. He always shot to the left. We held our breath, waiting for the last approach. Bobby jigged on the spot. Paul ran up.

He swung, and kicked.
Bobby dived left. The
ball powered to the
right, and into the
back of the goal.

Everyone gasped. Bobby
blinked, and rubbed his eyes.
Then he slumped into a heap,
burying his head in his lap.

My heart sank. Bobby was going
to refuse to budge, and no one
would be able to get home. We'd
be stuck at camp for ever and ever.

Paul rocked from foot to foot, not looking at Bobby, but inching closer. I thought I heard a soft humming of a familiar tune. I couldn't work out where it was coming from. But Bobby instantly looked up. His eyes widened. Then he walked up to Paul. Holding out his potato print bag, he announced: "Man o' the match, Paul!" A tiny smile played on Paul's mouth.

All too soon it was time to leave. The sun shone, but Paul had his coat back on. He pulled the hood down and flicked his zip, faster and faster. He didn't like the coach, and I suddenly realized how he felt: all trapped like a player being man-marked. He shot little glances around, a striker searching out a space.

"Awright, Paul?" Bobby sensed the unhappiness too. I could tell by the look on his face that he was trying to think of something to cheer Paul up. Looking for a distraction, he said: "'S my birthday soon, Paul."

Paul twiddled his coat toggles.

"July the thirtieth."

"The day England won the World Cup," I said proudly.

A soft voice added: "1966, Wembley, England 4, Germany 2."

The voice came from somewhere deep inside a hood!

"'S right. Wembley!" Bobby whooped.

I wanted to whoop, too: Paul was talking!

The whole coach fell silent.

"What about 1994?" Tom said.

"1994, USA," the soft voice from the coat continued. "Brazil 3, Italy 2. Penalties."

"34?" Jacob asked.

"June 10th, Italy. Italy 2, Czechoslovakia 1," Paul chanted.

Dates and times poured out in a rich river of words.

Bobby's eyes shone as he watched and listened.

All too soon we drew up in the school playground. Paul rushed for the coach door, rocking from foot to foot as he waited to be let out. Bobby tried to follow, but people blocked the gangway. He stood on his seat and yelled, "'Bye, Paul, 'bye!"

As the doors hissed open I watched a coat hood, trimmed with fur, nodding.

Then, very softly, from deep inside, I heard the words, "Wembley, 1966, Bobby, Charlton," and after a short pause, "Friends!"

And Bobby and I chorused back, "FRIENDS!"

Team Trouble

For my sisters,
Mary-Clare, Kate and Rachel – S.S

Chapter 1

"Come on, you reds!" Dad yelled.

Wembley balanced boots on his head, Striker kicked a cushion, Bobby shouted "Save," and Mum blew her whistle. It's always mad at our house on match days.

Everyone was ready. Everyone except Semi.

My middle brother was still in his pyjamas, sprawled across the sofa.

Bobby tugged his hand. "Get dress' NOW," he ordered.

But Semi just flicked through the channels, changing from a football match to a cartoon. Something was wrong. Very wrong. No one in our house ever switches the football off. And we always go to the match together – like Dad says, we're a team.

Mum and Dad exchanged glances, as if they knew something, but weren't telling.

Nobody spoke as we left. There was a big hole where Semi should have been.

Dad sang louder than usual, as if to fill the gap.

Semi wasn't around to tell jokes, so Bobby started: "Knock knock."

"Who's there?"

"Football!"

"Football who?"

"Football hoooligan!"

When our team won 3-0, and the crowd went wild, I thought of Semi. I couldn't remember him missing a match before, ever.

Next day, when I got home from school the house was strangely quiet. Mum wasn't singing, or dribbling a football round the kitchen. She was staring into space. My big brother, Striker, made her a cup of tea. I curled up in a corner with a football magazine. If I listened, I'd find out what the matter was.

"I think Semi's got your old disease," Mum said.

"What's that?" asked Striker.

"TT syndrome," she replied, ruffling his hair.

TT syndrome – what was that? I've always known my brother, Bobby, has Down's syndrome. That's why he goes to a different school from me. A special school. But he's not ill or anything, and he's a brilliant goalie. Now it looked like we had another syndrome in the family. This new one was really serious: it meant not liking football!

Chapter 2

Semi's TT syndrome didn't get better. It got worse. He wouldn't get up in the morning. He shouted at Bobby, and he started spending time in the bathroom. Semi hated baths; he never washed. But now he was locking himself away for hours.

"Come out NOW!" Bobby ordered. He missed playing with Semi.

"Go away!" Semi growled.

Bobby didn't know about the TTs, but he realized that something was wrong, and he moped for the old Semi – the one who told him daft jokes and wrestled with him.

One day, Semi arrived late to the meal. His hair was covered in gel, and sticking out.

"Look – a jelly hedgehog," Dad joked.

Mum shot him a warning glance. I was getting used to her noisy, silent stares.

"They'll be playing the new striker tomorrow." Dad tried to bring Semi out of his scowls. "D'you reckon he'll score?"

"Whatever," Semi shrugged.

The meal table went quiet. Our house is never quiet.

Semi hunched over his plate, shovelling food in.

"Don't eat with your mouth open," Dad said.

"Stop nagging me!" Semi flung down his knife and fork, slamming the door as he stormed out.

Dad stood up. "Semi . . ." he roared.

"Shhh," Mum stopped him. "Let it go – he needs lots of TLC at the moment."

"Yup – plenty of TLC for the old TTs." Dad looked fed up.

Well, I was fed up with grown-ups talking in code.

"Pass the TK," I said, pointing at the ketchup, "and the S and P."

I wasn't going to be left out.

Bobby plopped a sausage in the water jug, flicked a dollop of mashed potato at the ceiling, and muttered "ABC an' BBC".

Then he ate with his mouth wide open, deliberately putting out his tongue and showing us his half-eaten food.

"Bobby!" Mum snapped, flashing a yellow card. "Any more of that, and you'll be sent off."

"'S not fair," Bobby grumbled. "Give Semi a red card."

His face drooped till his nose pinged the gravy. Lifting his head, he grinned at me, then bobbed down for another go.

"That's enough," a deep voice growled.

"'Nuff B-U-M," Bobby muttered, before cramming three forkfuls into his mouth. If he was going to be sent off, he wasn't going to leave any of his chicken on the pitch!

Strangely, Mum didn't bring out the red card. She looked worried and a bit far away.

While I was washing up, I heard her talking softly with Dad. The word "doctor" set my ears jangling.

Later, Mum and Semi went out. Semi was wearing dark glasses, his hair flopped over his face like a pair of curtains. He was all hunched over. Whatever it was, it was getting worse.

When they came home, I saw him take a packet of pills from the shopping bag and slip them into his pocket.

"What're you staring at?" he snapped.

"Nothing." I sloped off into the garden. Kicking a football around usually makes me feel better.

But the funny feeling didn't go away. It grew.

So next day at school, I sneaked a look in the big dictionary. First, I searched for "Sindrome". Whatever Semi had, it was something bad. Sins were bad. But it wasn't under sin. Eventually, I found the word under S Y N, and read:

"Combination of behaviour and emotions." Well, Semi was certainly showing some odd behaviour recently. But then, Dad and Mum have some odd behaviour, and they didn't have syndromes. At least, I didn't think they did. It was confusing. I read the next bit: "Symptoms of a disease," it said. That sounded more serious. Doctor. Pills. Semi must be poorly. What if he was really ill?

Chapter 3

I kept looking out for signs of
Semi's illness. But it wasn't like a
normal illness, when you go to bed
for a few days and then get better.
Instead, he came down stairs, lay
on the sofa, and grunted at people.

"D'you want to read my
football magazine?"

"Ooof."

"I want to watch the other
channel."

"Noyoucan't. Oof."

"Come to the park with us,
Semi."

"Naagarroffanleavemealone.
Oof!"

One day Mum took him
shopping. When we're poorly
Mum buys us little treats – drinks
and comics. But Semi came back
with a whole bag of new clothes.
So whatever it was, TT must be
more serious than chickenpox.

The clothes were awful. We all wear football shirts, but Semi's new shirt was was covered in flowers – ugh! Dad got out his watering can and started to sprinkle the flowery shirt. Mum shooed him away. He stomped out like a player who's been sent off.

Semi's bedroom changed, as well as his clothes. All the football posters came down, and up went pictures of girls in bikinis.

He's always loved swimming (not like me) but when Mum suggested he take Bobby to the pool, he just grunted.

"Don'wanto. Oof."

"Go on, it'll do you good – and

you, Charlie." Mum swooshed us all out of the house.

At the pool, Bobby made straight for the diving board. He bounced up and down, then launched himself into space, arms and legs flying. As he flew off the board, I threw a ball at him. He kicked it back, yelled, "Goal!" and disappeared into a mass of bubbles.

I liked this game – it meant I didn't have to get into the water at all. But after a while I got bored, and wanted to read a book. Semi was lying in the sun, so I went to sit near him. A dripping Bobby followed and gave Semi a wet hug.

"Geroff," he growled.

"Play polo?" Bobby asked.

Semi's brilliant at water polo, and usually he and Bobby play for hours. But today Bobby got the 'Go away' treatment.

So he played on his own for a bit, before crumpling next to Semi. Like me, he was confused.

And cross.

Semi lay on the grass, not reading, not talking, not doing anything. And he wouldn't take off that horrible shirt. I tried to ignore him. But Bobby kept fluttering round with questions – "Wha' you doin'?" "Why?" "Why don' you want to swim?"

Perhaps he'd become allergic to water, I thought. Naomi in my class is allergic to nuts. And Daniel has a special pen in case he gets stung by bees. But if Semi was allergic to water, why did he spend hours in the bathroom? It didn't make sense.

Bobby got fed up. A few minutes later, he crept towards Semi carrying a cup of water. He lifted up the flowery shirt, and was just about to pour water onto his back when he shrieked and ran away.

"Ugh! Yukky, yukky!" Bobby pointed in disgust.

Semi leaped to his feet, furious. He picked Bobby up, chucked

him into the pool, and stormed
off.

I stared after him. So, the
secret TT disease was on his
back. Bobby had seen it. And it
was horrible. More horrible than
I'd ever imagined.

Chapter 4

Bobby was upset. He knew that
Semi was really angry, and kept
trying to make it better.

"Wanta sweet?" he offered.
"Carry your bag, Semi?"

"Knock, knock, who's there?"

But Semi ignored him all the
way home.

When we got back, Bobby kept
trying to be nice to Semi. "Cuppa
tea?" he asked. "Borrow my goalie

video?" But Semi didn't even look up. Then he offered Semi a football sticker – not just any sticker, but his best one, the one with his goalie hero, Will Brooks. "For you . . ." he said.

Semi just grunted and pushed him away. Finally, Bobby buried his head in his crossed legs and wouldn't say a word. Perhaps he was catching TT syndrome too, I thought. Maybe we'd all get it, and everyone in the house would stop talking, and just grunt. Perhaps tourists would come and visit The House of Grunts.

I kicked a ball around listlessly till tea time.

When Bobby sat down he had

his "I've been up to something"
look on his face. Mum usually
notices it straightaway, and I
waited for her to tackle him. But
she just dished out the mashed
potato – one scoop on each plate,
and then one dollop in the gold-
fish bowl.

"Mum!"

"Oh, silly me – I was miles
away."

Goal Fish nudged the potato
ball down the tank.

"He's making a run on goal," I said.

No one laughed. Then the door burst open. Semi grabbed Bobby and pulled him roughly onto the floor. Semi, my gentle, dreamy brother, started hitting Bobby.

Mum blew a whistle. "Stop at once," she said, flashing a red card.

Semi gasped and yelled, "He's scribbled all over my pictures. I hate this place and I hate this family. I'm leaving!"

He stormed out.

"Rude boy," Bobby muttered, and scuttled under the table.

Mum and Dad exchanged glances, and I wondered what they'd do. They hate fighting, and always try to teach me to hold my head up high and walk away when I'm angry. But they'd never had to say that to Semi.

I expected Dad to go after Semi and be really fierce, but Mum gave him one of her signals and he stayed where he was.

"Bobby!" she said. "Upstairs. Now."

I sneaked up behind them, and peeped round the door as Mum marched Bobby into Semi's room.

Bobby hung his head as Mum pointed to the posters. All the smiling, bikini-clad girls now had football shirts and bobble hats. Felt pens were scattered over the floor. He'd even pinned a smelly old sock onto one girl's belly button.

There was a long silence. Then a great crashing sound came from the garden. We all rushed to the window. A bucket flew out of the shed. An old bike wheel rolled after it, and wobbled its way into the cabbages. Dad stood and watched as the entire contents of his beloved shed flew onto the grass. He looked shocked, like a ref who's just had a ball kicked in his face.

An arm reached round the shed door, and a notice appeared: "Private! Keep Out!"

We all stared at each other, stunned.

Semi had left home.

Chapter 5

Poor Semi. He was ill, and alone. I remembered a nature programme I'd seen, when the old animal left the herd to die.

I tried to imagine how I'd feel if I was really poorly, and someone drew on my football posters, and I had to go and sleep in a shed with snails and spiders. I wanted my brother back, and I wanted him better. Mum always says, "When you're sad, try and think of something that will make someone else happy."

My piggy bank stared at me.

I'd got just enough saved to buy the last footballer for my team. I really wanted that model.

But Semi was poorly.

I could have the whole set.

But what if Semi was ill, really ill?

I rattled Piggy. All my pocket money. And it was Bobby who'd

scribbled on the posters, not me –
why should I do anything?

Piggy seemed to shake his head
– as if he was telling me that our
family team was more important
than a plastic one. Reluctantly, I
carried the money box out to the
shed.

I pictured his smiling face. I'd
be the one to bring him home. I'd
help him get better.

I knocked on the door, and
said, "Semi, here's some money
to buy new posters."

"Gerrroff and goaway!" Semi
yelled.

Chapter 6

That was it. He could go on a free transfer to Dirty Shed United for all I cared!

I stormed inside. It was worse than the day we lost the Cup Final. I'd tried really hard to be kind, and he'd slammed the door in my face!

Well, he'd asked for it.

"Mum," I began, "we need a baby."

She spluttered tea everywhere.

"A new midfielder."

Mum rattled her cup down.
"There's only one midfielder in
this family," she said fiercely,
"and that's Semi! He's my middle
child, and right now he's in the
middle of some troubles."

"Piggy 'n middle, piggy 'n
muddle," Bobby sang from under
the sofa.

"That's enough from you, young man – it's time you went and said sorry. Off you go. You can take him his tea."

Bobby picked up Semi's plate. Then he stopped. He was trying to decide something. Finally, he sighed, took the lolly from his mouth, and popped it on top of the potato.

A hand reached out from the shed door, and took the plate.

There was a grunt, "Oof". The door closed. Then it opened again. A lolly flew out and hit Bobby – smack – on the nose!

Chapter 7

Semi stayed in the shed. He only came indoors to lock himself in the bathroom for hours. And more hours. Then, smelling like a flower shop, he'd leave. He never said where he was going or when he'd be back, and I could tell that bothered Mum, even though she didn't say anything.

"Me come?" Bobby asked each time.

And each time he was greeted with a big "NO". So Bobby would go and mope under the sofa. I tried to coax him out to play football, but he just shook his head and buried his face in the carpet. I ended up all alone, kicking a ball against the back wall. It felt like I'd lost two brothers.

One day Semi went out.

"An' me?" Bobby tried.

Semi left without answering,

and I saw a new look on Bobby's face. He lay under the sofa, but his eyes peeped out from between his fingers. He was up to something. I went into the kitchen and listened. Soft footsteps made their way to the front door. It closed very quietly. I peered out, and watched Bobby tiptoeing down the road like a pantomime villain, as Semi disappeared into the distance.

Jumping into my trainers, I rushed after them.

The sky darkened.

I jumped from tree to tree. Semi kept stopping, looking round nervously. A cat darted out. Semi jumped. What was turning my big, brave brother into this jittery ghost? A car with black windows snaked up to the kerb. It slid away like a shark, and Semi scuttled down an alley. He started to run. This wasn't just an illness. He was frightened of something.

I couldn't see Bobby. I froze.

A group approached, and Semi dived out of sight. They passed me, and I recognized them from Semi's class. Why was he hiding from his schoolmates?

There was a rumble of

thunder, and heavy rain drops began to fall. Dark spots appeared on Semi's shirt, merging and clinging to his hunched shape. Something screeched from the bushes. Branches whipped my face and the path became a black tunnel. Semi moved faster. He looked around again, then darted through a gap in the hedge.

Seconds later, I squeezed after him, into the park. It was empty. Deserted. If someone attacked him, no one would hear his screams. Lightning slashed the sky, and he ran towards it, taking great loping strides as if he was being chased. I darted from bush to bush, losing him and glimpsing

him again as he sprinted like the wind. There was just one, solitary figure in the bandstand, something dark pulled over its head. Was it armed? Semi pounded forwards. He raised his arms towards the figure. Thunder rolled around the park, and the two shapes fell together, and disappeared from sight. Someone had grabbed him.

Chapter 8

Who'd got Semi? And where was Bobby? I charged forward.

A bloodcurdling noise erupted from the hollyhocks.

A head shot up.

"OOOooh – kissy, kissy, kissy!" Bobby's grin appeared from a flowerbed.

Semi sprang to his feet, his face a red card. I could feel his glare fifty metres away.

Sitting beside him, surprised and fluffy, was a girl. A girly girl!

Looking up, she fluttered, and reached out for Semi. She was holding my brother's hand! Staring up at him with a silly, soppy expression on her face.

"Play foo'ball?" Bobby's voice wobbled.

"Go away!" Semi hissed.

Bobby put his head on one side and held out the ball.

"Foo'ball, please?" His small voice floated from the flowers.

The wispy, golden hair twirled towards Semi and back to Bobby.

"P'ease?"

"Go home!" Semi pointed furiously at the gate.

"I'll play, Bobby," I tried.

"Semi . . ." Bobby wailed.

"Come on. Let's go." Semi tugged the girl. She tottered beside him for a few steps in her wibbly wobbly shoes. Then she stopped.

"Hold this." She thrust a sparkly handbag at Semi and teetered towards the flowerbed. Bobby held out the football and said, "For you," as if it was a present.

She took the ball and trip trapped onto the pitch, nearly falling off her stupid shoes. She tried to kick but missed. I smiled. Then Bobby passed her another one, really gently. She sliced it badly.

"Goo' girl," he said when she returned it, and then asked, "Name?"

"Primrose," she replied.

"Premier," Bobby nodded, passing the ball back to her. Her heels slipped down into the mud. She unstrapped the shoes, put them neatly together, and skipped into a puddle. Clumsily, she kicked the ball back to Bobby,

squelching and giggling across the muddy pitch.

Semi and I stood on the touchline and stared at each other. Finally, Bobby said, "Tea time, Premier!" and taking her by the hand, he led the way to our house.

Semi picked up her shoes and sulked along behind. I joined him, taking his free hand. "She'll never go out with me again if she sees our house and you lot," Semi said miserably. I didn't like the way he called us "you lot", but he had spoken to me, in real words and without a single grunt. And he hadn't pushed my hand away.

"Don't worry," I said. "She's nice."

And for the first time in weeks, he smiled at me.

We reached our house, and Mum opened the door. A cabbage sailed over her head, and a rather startled Primrose Premier caught it.

"Goo' save," Bobby said, and led her inside.

Chapter 9

It was match day again. Everyone was getting ready – well, everyone except Semi.

The door bell rang, and Bobby ran to open it, yelling, "Primrose Premier!"

Tugging her hand, he dragged her through to the garden.

"Penalties?" he asked, handing her a football.

Bobby usually does penalty

practice with me. I kicked a cushion at the wall. Nobody even noticed me.

Mum wandered in singing, "Football's coming home, it's coming . . ."

She gazed happily at Bobby and Primrose in the garden, then said, "Semi's a lucky lad."

"Is he?" I looked up, startled.

"Yes," Mum smiled. "She's a lovely girl. You wanted a new midfielder. I think she's a great new signing, don't you?"

"She kicks like a girl," I said. Then added, "And I bet he hasn't told her about his illness."

"What illness?" Mum looked puzzled.

"You know. The doctor. All that stuff. You and Dad never telling him off. His yukky back . . ."

"Oh, Charlie," she laughed, "that was just spots, acne. Lots of teenagers get it. It's nearly gone now."

"Oh, I thought . . . I was

worried he might . . ." my voice
wobbled.

Then Dad appeared yelling
"Nearly match time – come on,
you reds!"

"And yellows," Bobby added,
thundering upstairs and shouting,
"Get up, Semi slug-a-bed!"

Primrose trotted behind him, saying, "Hurry up, Semi – you promised you'd take me to my first match."

Striker came in, grinning, and said, "Semi seems to be getting over the TTs."

"What's that?" I demanded.

"Oh, just Teenage Troubles, dear," Mum said. "You'll have them too."

"I won't. I won't ever stop liking football!" I said.

"I'm afraid you will," Mum smiled, "and then you'll need some extra TLC, just like Semi."

"You're doing it again!"

"What?" asked Mum.

"Talking in code. What's TLC?"

"Tender Loving Care," Mum, Dad and Striker said together.

"Youngest children need that too," I grumped, "and a syndrome. I don't want to be the only person in this house without a syndrome."

"An' me," said Bobby.

"Bobby, you can have BIGS," said Mum. "Best In Goal!"

"Charlie's got BOGSS," Dad added. "Brilliant Only Girl Striker Syndrome!"

"Football, BIGS?" I asked.

"Yes, BOGSS," Bobby replied.

"Wait for us!" Semi and Primrose bounded out. "We'll give you a game!"